Dear Parent:
Your child's love of reading starts here!

Every child learns to read in a different way and at his or her own speed. Some go back and forth between reading levels and read favorite books again and again. Others read through each level in order. You can help your young reader improve and become more confident by encouraging his or her own interests and abilities. From books your child reads with you to the first books he or she reads alone, there are I Can Read Books for every stage of reading:

SHARED READING
Basic language, word repetition, and whimsical illustrations, ideal for sharing with your emergent reader

BEGINNING READING
Short sentences, familiar words, and simple concepts for children eager to read on their own

READING WITH HELP
Engaging stories, longer sentences, and language play for developing readers

READING ALONE
Complex plots, challenging vocabulary, and high-interest topics for the independent reader

ADVANCED READING
Short paragraphs, chapters, and exciting themes for the perfect bridge to chapter books

I Can Read Books have introduced children to the joy of reading since 1957. Featuring award-winning authors and illustrators and a fabulous cast of beloved characters, I Can Read Books set the standard for beginning readers.

A lifetime of discovery begins with the magical words "I Can Read!"

Visit www.icanread.com for information
on enriching your child's reading experience.

ADVENTURES OF SUPERMAN™

Justice League Classic: Meet the Justice League
Copyright © 2013 by DC Comics.
JUSTICE LEAGUE and all related characters and elements
are trademarks of and © DC Comics.
(s13)

HARP29086

Superman Classic: Escape from the Phantom Zone
Copyright © 2011 by DC Comics.
BATMAN, SUPERMAN, WONDER WOMAN, and all related
characters and elements are trademarks of and © DC Comics.
(s11)

HARP13252

Superman Classic: Superman versus the Silver Banshee
Copyright © 2013 by DC Comics.
SUPERMAN and all related characters and elements are
trademarks of and © DC Comics.
(s13)

HARP2642

Superman Classic: Day of Doom
Copyright © 2013 by DC Comics.
SUPERMAN and all related characters and elements are
trademarks of and © DC Comics.
(s13)

HARP28603

ISBN 978-1-4351-5063-8

Manufactured in Dong Guan City, China
Lot #:
16 17 18 19 SCP 5 4
09/16

I Can Read!™

ADVENTURES OF SUPERMAN™

Superman created by Jerry Siegel and Joe Shuster
By special arrangement with the Jerry Siegel family

HARPER

An Imprint of HarperCollinsPublishers

Table of Contents

Meet the Justice League

by Lucy Rosen

pictures by Steven E. Gordon

colors by Eric A. Gordon

SUPERMAN

Superman has many amazing powers. He was born on the planet Krypton.

BATMAN

Batman fights crime in Gotham City. He wears a mask and a cape.

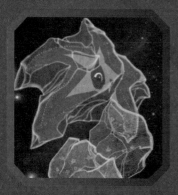

STARRO

A titanic, intergalactic starfish that hungers for universal conquest.

WONDER WOMAN

One of the strongest beings on the planet, Wonder Woman is an expert at all forms of combat.

THE FLASH

Known as the Scarlet Speedster, the Flash can run at near lightspeed after a science experiment gone awry granted him the power to tap into the Speed Force.

AQUAMAN

The King of Atlantis is a member of the Justice League. He can breathe underwater and possesses healing powers as well as other magical abilities.

MARTIAN MANHUNTER

A member of the Justice League, Martian Manhunter's powers include super-strength, shape-shifting, and the ability to fire energy beams from his eyes.

GREEN LANTERN

Green Lantern helped found the Justice League, alongside Aquaman and the Flash. Wearing his power ring allows him to travel through space.

Today Clark Kent

was going to interview

the police chief of Metropolis.

But when Clark went to the station,

he knew something was wrong.

All the cops were standing still.

No one moved an inch.

A cop looked at Clark

with a strange, blank stare.

"I know that look," said Clark.

He turned the cop around.

There was a small starfish

stuck to the back of his neck!

Clark checked all the cops.

Everyone had a starfish!

"Starro!" he cried.

Clark knew he had to act.

"This looks like a job for Superman!"

Superman had faced Starro before.
The evil alien starfish
could take over anyone's mind.
He was a powerful enemy.
And this time, Starro had
even more people under control!

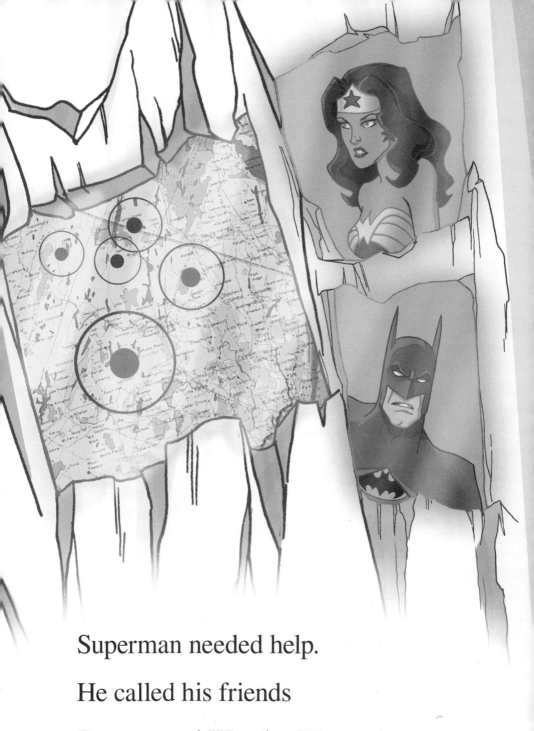

Superman needed help.

He called his friends

Batman and Wonder Woman.

But Starro had struck their cities, too!

"Starro cloned himself and sent his legion
to destroy our cities," said Batman.
"To stop him, we'll need help!"
Wonder Woman knew just who to call.
A few minutes later,
Superman, Batman, and Wonder Woman
were together with some new friends.

The Flash could run faster
than anyone on Earth.
Aquaman had the power
to swim deep into the ocean
without ever getting tired.
Martian Manhunter
could read people's thoughts.
And with his power ring,
Green Lantern could create
anything he could imagine.

"This is a big job," said Superman.
"We must defeat the clones,
then we have to find Starro
and stop him for good."

The super heroes agreed
to split up into teams.

Superman and the Flash
zoomed back to Metropolis.
The brainwashed cops
were all over the city!

"I'll round them up," said the Flash.

"Be back in a second."

In the blink of an eye,

the Flash returned with all

the officers together!

23

Superman breathed in deeply.
One by one, he froze the starfish
with his icy breath.
The Flash circled around and
gathered the frozen clones.

"That was quick,"

the two speedy super heroes

laughed together.

The Flash and Superman
raced to Gotham City.
Batman had found all the
clones with his Batcomputer.
Between the Flash's speed,
Superman's freeze breath,
and Batman's combat skills,
they had the clones collected
in no time.

Meanwhile, in Washington, DC,
Green Lantern used his power ring
to find and gather the cops.
Wonder Woman snared one
in her Lasso of Truth.

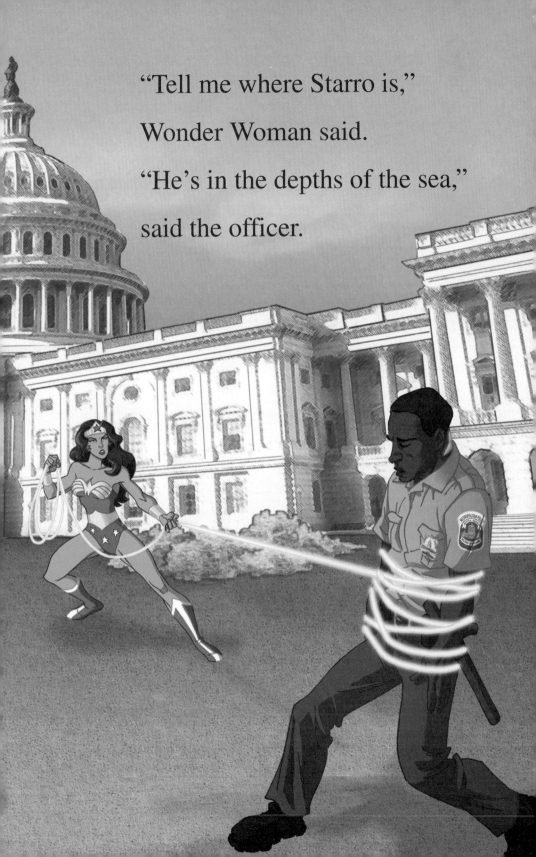

"Tell me where Starro is,"
Wonder Woman said.
"He's in the depths of the sea,"
said the officer.

"We'll see about that,"

said Wonder Woman.

"Martian Manhunter, do you copy?"

she said in her mind.

"Got it," said Martian Manhunter.

He and Wonder Woman

had linked minds.

"Time to hit the beach,"

the alien hero told Aquaman.

Martian Manhunter sent
the rest of the super heroes
a mental message.
They all met at the edge of the ocean.

Aquaman dived into the water.
He swam as fast as a shark.
There, in the murky depths
of the ocean,
he found the vile starfish.

Aquaman grabbed Starro

by an arm and pulled him up.

Green Lantern used his ring

to help lift Starro out of the ocean.

Superman froze the villain
with his icy breath.

35

"Time to get rid of this pest,"
said Martian Manhunter.
He and Superman
grabbed Starro and the clones
and flew them to outer space.
Superman used his super-breath
to scatter the starfish
all over the galaxy!

Back on Earth,

the super heroes celebrated.

"Nothing like teamwork to keep

the planet safe!" Batman said.

SUPERMAN™

Escape from the Phantom Zone

by John Sazaklis
pictures by Steven E. Gordon

SUPERMAN created by Jerry Siegel and Joe Shuster

BATMAN created by Bob Kane

WONDER WOMAN created by William Moulton Marston

SUPERMAN

Superman was born on the planet Krypton and sent to Earth. Earth's yellow sun gives Superman many amazing powers.

BATMAN

Batman lives in Gotham City. He is an expert crime fighter with an arsenal of cutting-edge equipment.

WONDER WOMAN

Wonder Woman was born on Paradise Island. She is an Amazon Princess and fierce warrior.

GENERAL ZOD

Zod is a power-hungry madman from Krypton. Superman's father sent Zod to the Phantom Zone for his violent crimes.

NON & URSA

Non and Ursa are Zod's loyal followers. They helped Zod escape from the Phantom Zone once.

THE PHANTOM ZONE

The Phantom Zone is an outer-space prison that holds some of the universe's most dangerous criminals.

Superman is in his secret hideout,
the Fortress of Solitude,
when an alarm goes off.
Superman calls his friends
Batman and Wonder Woman.

"My readings show something dangerous

is headed toward Metropolis,"

Superman says.

"We must work together to stop it."

The heroes meet in Metropolis.

"Everything seems fine," Batman says.

"Are you sure there's a problem?"

"Trust me," Superman replies.

Suddenly, a portal opens in the sky
and three strange people appear.
"We seek the one called Superman!"
the leader yells.

"Do you know them?" Batman asks.

"Yes, they are dangerous criminals

from my home planet,"

Superman says.

"We must protect the city!"

shouts Wonder Woman.

"Be careful," Superman warns.

"Here on Earth, they have

the same special powers that I do!"

"I am General Zod," shouts the leader.
"We have escaped the Phantom Zone,
where your father imprisoned us.
Now we will get our revenge, Superman."

"Once Superman is taken care of,"
Ursa says, "we will rule this silly planet.
Humans will be our pets!"

"Earth is my home now," Superman says.

"And I have sworn to protect it.

You are not welcome here!"

"We will crush you!" General Zod cries.

In a flash, he attacks Superman.

The heroes must help their friend.

Batman charges at Non,

but the villain uses his super-breath

to freeze Batman in his tracks.

Ursa blasts Wonder Woman
with her heat vision.
Wonder Woman blocks the beams
with her magic bracelets.

Superman fears that the battle

will harm innocent people.

General Zod holds Superman in his grip.

"You are no match for us," Zod says.

Superman comes up with a plan
and looks at his friends.

He cannot tell them his idea.

He trusts they will follow his lead.

The Man of Steel breaks free

and takes off into the air.

"Catch me if you can!" he yells.

The three villains chase Superman.

He flies to the Fortress of Solitude.

That is where Superman keeps

the Phantom Zone Projector.

It is a special machine that can send

villains back to the Phantom Zone!

Batman and Wonder Woman
follow close behind
in Wonder Woman's Invisible Jet.
They see Superman and the villains
enter the Fortress of Solitude.

"Superman is distracting them
so we can plan a sneak attack,"
Batman says.

"Let's hurry," Wonder Woman replies.

"Before it's too late!"

Zod is impressed with the Fortress.

"This can be our throne room," he says.

"Look, the Phantom Zone Projector!"

Ursa says, pointing to the machine.

"Let's use it on Superman!"

"First things first," says the general.
"Superman will kneel before Zod!"
The villains combine their heat vision,
forcing Superman to his knees.

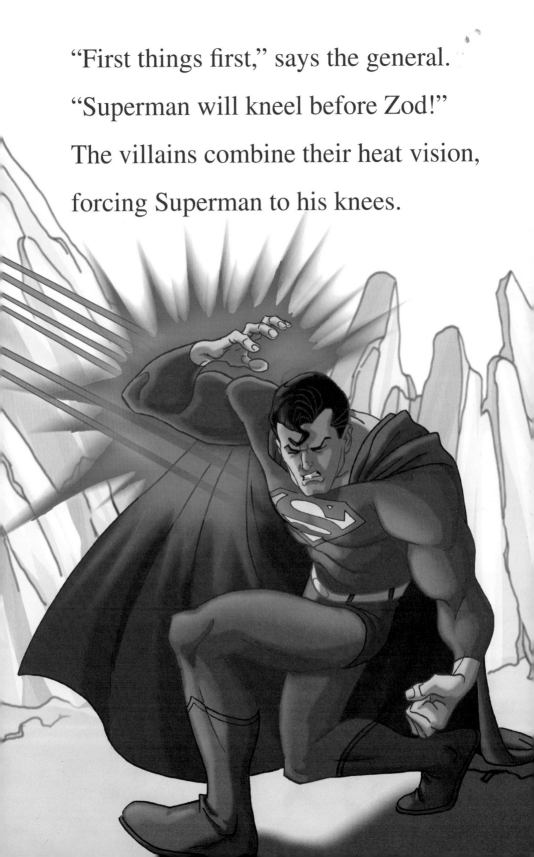

The hidden heroes leap into action!
Wonder Woman ties up Non and Ursa
with her magic Lasso of Truth.
"How do we send you back?"
Wonder Woman asks.

The lasso forces the villains

to tell the truth.

"The Phantom Zone Projector," they say.

"It will send us back to prison."

Batman races to turn on the machine.

Zod is distracted by the sneak attack.

"You fools," he yells at Ursa and Non.

"Work together! Do not let them win!"

Superman jumps up and says,

"Game over, General. You lose!"

Then he throws Zod into the machine.

Batman flips the switch.

A laser beam blasts General Zod.

"Curse you, Superman!" Zod cries

as he begins to fade away.

Wonder Woman throws Non and Ursa
into the projector's path.
They follow their leader all the way
back to the Phantom Zone!

"Thank you," Superman says.
"We sure showed Zod and his gang
what teamwork really means!"

versus the
Silver Banshee

by Donald Lemke
pictures by Andy Smith

CLARK KENT

Clark Kent is a
newspaper reporter.
He is secretly Superman.

LOIS LANE

Lois Lane is a
reporter. She works
for the *Daily Planet*
newspaper.

SUPERMAN

Superman has
many amazing powers.
He was born on the planet
Krypton.

LEX LUTHOR

Lex Luthor is a wealthy Metropolis businessman. He is Superman's enemy.

SILVER BANSHEE

Silver Banshee is the daughter of a powerful Gaelic clan leader. An evil witch gave her magic superpowers.

S.T.A.R. LABS

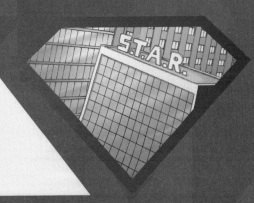

S.T.A.R. Labs is a research center in Metropolis.

Siobhan McDougal was the daughter of a powerful clan leader.
After her father's death, she tried taking over the clan but failed.
She was sent to live in the underworld.

Then one day, Siobhan met
an evil witch known as the Crone.
The witch promised to help her
return to the land of the living.

The Crone gave Siobhan superpowers and named her Silver Banshee.

In exchange for these gifts,

the witch asked for a magical old book.

It had belonged to Silver Banshee's father.

"Bring me the book," said the witch,

"or your powers will be lost."

Silver Banshee agreed to the task.

"Nothing will stop me!" she said.

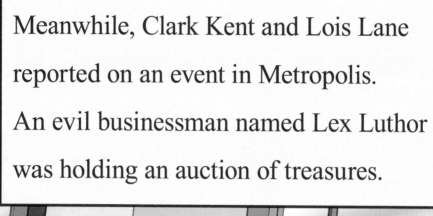

Meanwhile, Clark Kent and Lois Lane reported on an event in Metropolis. An evil businessman named Lex Luthor was holding an auction of treasures.

Lex held up the final item for sale that day.

The crowd gasped at the rare book.

"Let's start the bidding at

one million dollars!" Lex said.

"Who would pay that price
for an old book?" Lois asked Clark.
But Clark wasn't listening.
His super-hearing had picked up
a strange sound outside.

SMASH! Silver Banshee suddenly burst into the room.

"That book's not for sale," she shouted.

"It's mine!"

79

"This news story just
got interesting," said Lois.
She turned to Clark,
but he was nowhere to be found.

Out of sight, Clark shed his suit.

"This looks like a job

for Superman!" he said.

WHOOSH! The Man of Steel

soared back into the room.

"Give up!" Superman shouted

at Silver Banshee.

"Not until I've had the last word!"

said the angry villain.

Silver Banshee let loose

a sonic scream.

Her magic powers stopped

Superman in midair.

As Superman regained his strength,

Silver Banshee returned to her evil task.

"Where is it?" the villain shouted.

Lex and the book were already gone!

"After I find that book, Superman, I'm coming back for you!" shouted Silver Banshee.

The villain fled into the night.

"My powers are useless

against magic," said Superman.

He flew toward S.T.A.R. Labs.

The research center built

tools to help super heroes.

"I have just the thing, Superman!"
said the lab's lead scientist.
He gave the hero a high-tech collar.
"If you put it on Silver Banshee
it will silence her scream,"
said the man.

Moments later, Superman arrived

in downtown Metropolis.

Silver Banshee was attacking

the LexCorp building.

She blasted the windows

with her sonic scream.

"Help, Superman!" Lex called out.

The evil businessman was trapped.

Superman was his only hope.

"I need to get close without
getting a splitting headache,"
said the Man of Steel.
He picked up a lead pipe
and broke it in half.

Superman molded the pieces into tiny lead earplugs! Silver Banshee spotted Superman. "Didn't you learn your lesson the first time?" she asked.

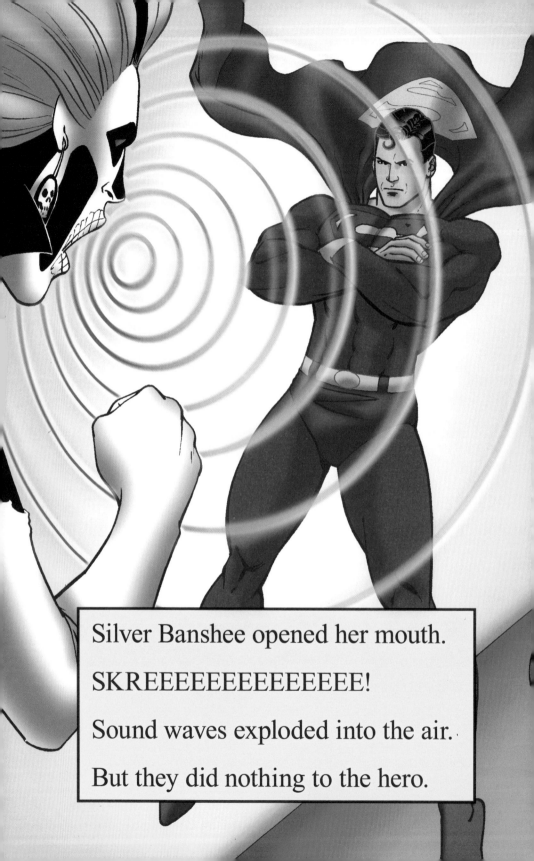

Silver Banshee opened her mouth.

SKREEEEEEEEEEEEEE!

Sound waves exploded into the air.

But they did nothing to the hero.

Superman used his heat vision.
The blazing hot beams knocked
Silver Banshee down.

"Try this on for size!" said Superman.

He placed the collar around her neck.

Silver Banshee pulled and pulled,

but the device was locked tight.

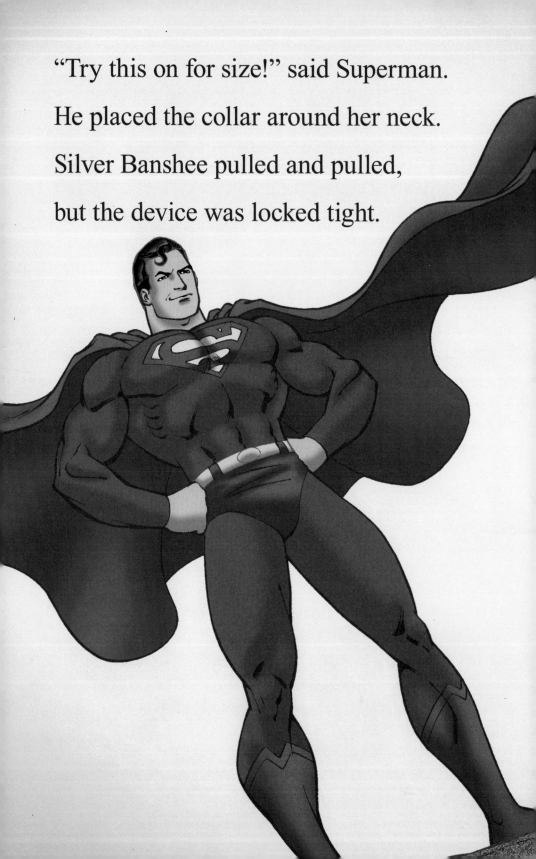

"It's no use!" said the Man of Steel.

"Even your magic can't break it."

Superman smiled.

"Well," he said, "any last words?"

Silver Banshee opened her mouth.

This time, the high-tech collar

kept her scream from escaping.

The evil power filled inside her

like a balloon about to burst.

The device turned

Silver Banshee's magic against her.

BOOOOM!

She blasted back to

the underworld!

Superman then soared toward Lex
and grabbed the book from him.

"You'll pay for that!" Lex shouted.

"Consider us even," Superman said
as he flew off to hide the book from evil.

Day of Doom

by John Sazaklis
pictures by Andy Smith
colors by Brad Vancata

SUPERMAN created by Jerry Siegel and Joe Shuster

CLARK KENT

Clark Kent is a
newspaper reporter.
He is secretly Superman.

LOIS LANE

Lois Lane is also a
newspaper reporter.
She works for the
Daily Planet newspaper.

JIMMY OLSEN

Jimmy Olsen is a
photographer. He works
with Clark and Lois for the
Daily Planet newspaper.

SUPERMAN

Superman has many amazing powers. He was born on the planet Krypton.

DOOMSDAY

The perfect killing machine, each time Doomsday is defeated, he comes back stronger than before.

Deep in an underground vault,

a monster struggles.

This alien criminal was imprisoned

to protect the people of Earth.

Now free, Doomsday sets off
on a path of destruction.
His targets are Metropolis
and its protector, Superman!

At the Daily Planet Building,

the news team is hard at work.

Suddenly, BOOM!

The walls begin to shake.

"What was that?" Lois asks.

Perry White exits his office.

"That's our front page story,"

he yells. "Go get it!"

Clark uses his X-ray vision.

He sees the cause of the rumble.

It is a large, rampaging creature!

Lois and Jimmy run to the elevator.

"Where are you going, Mr. Kent?"

Jimmy asks Clark.

"Elevators make me nervous,"

replies Clark. "I'll take the stairs."

With his friends gone,

Clark changes into his alter ego.

"This looks like a job for Superman!"

Doomsday tears through the city.

He stomps on cars with his feet.

He rips lampposts out of the ground.

In a blur of red and blue,

Superman appears.

"Your trail of terror ends here,"

says the Man of Steel.

Doomsday charges forward.

Superman attacks back.

The two titans clash but they are
equally matched.

"If I can't defeat this villain with strength," Superman says, "then I'll have to use speed!"

The Man of Steel breaks his grasp

and zips behind Doomsday.

He catches the villain off guard.

Superman punches Doomsday

into an abandoned parking garage.

The building collapses onto the beast.

KA-BOOM!

Lois and Jimmy run to Superman.

"You did it," Lois says.

"You saved the day!" Jimmy adds.

The young reporter snaps pictures.

Behind them, the rubble moves.

A massive fist rams through,

followed by the rest of Doomsday.

The monster roars with rage.

Doomsday leaps high into the air.
He lands on Superman and
pounds him into the pavement.
SMASH!

With the Man of Steel lost underground,

Doomsday turns to face the reporters.

"Uh-oh," Lois says. "RUN!"

She grabs Jimmy and sprints for safety.

Superman flies out of the crater

and sees his friends in danger.

"If strength and speed aren't enough,"

says the hero, "I'll have to use smarts."

He aims his heat vision

at the street, and he fires.

The asphalt begins to melt, and

Doomsday sinks into the street.

"Just returning the favor, big fella,"

Superman says to Doomsday.

Superman uses his freezing breath

to quickly cool the hot asphalt.

The monster is temporarily trapped.

"You need to chill out," says Superman.

Then he flies as fast as he can
to his Fortress of Solitude.
That is where the Man of Steel
keeps artifacts from his home planet.

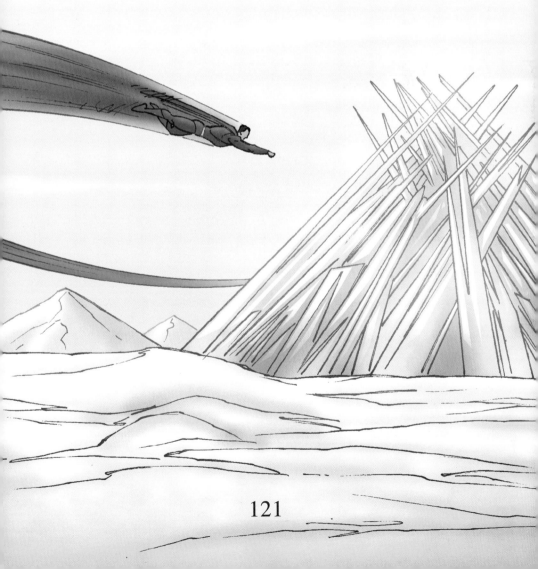

At the Fortress, Superman
picks up a special device.
It is the Phantom Zone Projector.
The Projector sends criminals to the
Phantom Zone, an outer space prison.

The Man of Steel then zooms

from the Arctic back to Metropolis.

In the city, Doomsday breaks free.

He heads for the Daily Planet Building.

Will Superman be too late?

Suddenly, Superman reappears!

"Your day of doom is over," he says.

He zaps Doomsday with the device.

In a flash, the villain is gone.

Lois and Jimmy thank Superman
for saving the city once again.
"It is my sworn duty,"
Superman says.

Then the hero waves and flies away.

Seconds later, Clark Kent

stumbles out of the Daily Planet Building.

"Phew! That building has WAY

too many stairs." Clark gasps.

"Did I miss anything?"

"You sure did, Clark," Lois says.

"Too bad you're not as fast

as Superman," Jimmy adds.

"Too bad," Clark says, and smiles.

"I bet you got a great story to tell!"